To my mother
who cleaned my footprints off
the ceiling many days with
patience and understanding

First published in the United States of America in 1992 by
Children's Universe
Rizzoli International Publications, Inc.
300 Park Avenue South, New York, New York 10010

Cataloging-in-Publication Data for this book is available from the
Library of Congress

92 93 94 95 96 / 10 9 8 7 6 5 4 3 2 1

Typographic design and consultation by Charles Kreloff

Printed in Hong Kong

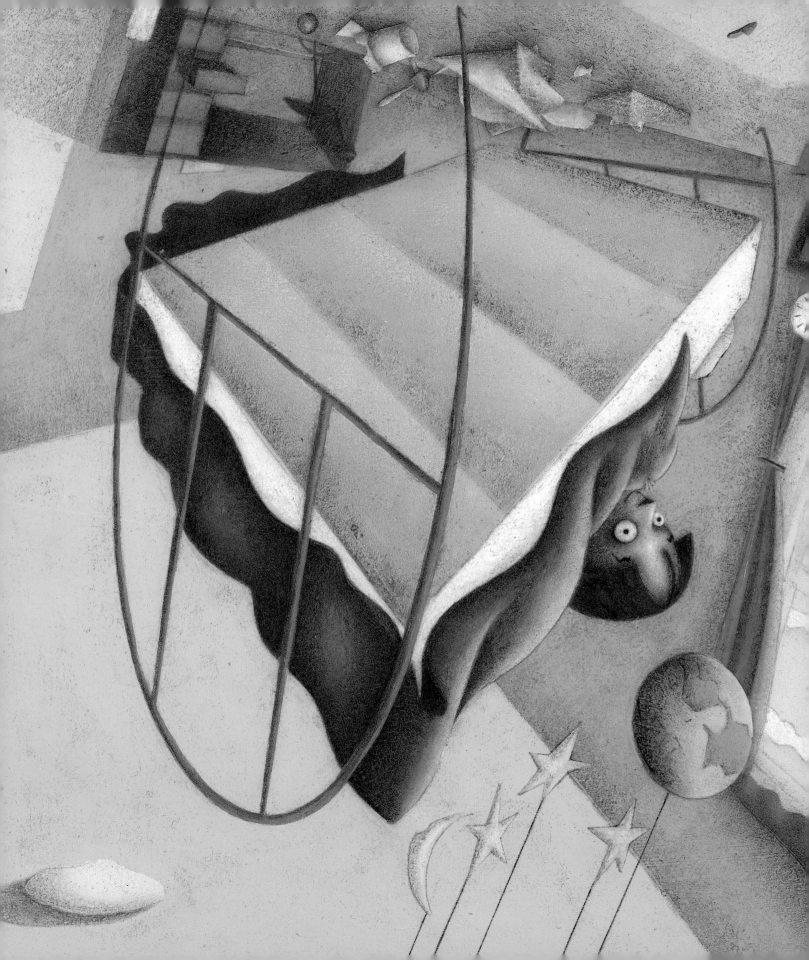

. . . to get up on the right side of the bed.

And what comes down will stay down until it gets up. And so he did. Only next time, he was much more careful when it was time for him to get up . . .

Now we know that what goes up, must come down,
And so little Moth did, eventually.

No ground, no sky, no in-between. Just him turning
'round and 'round. Right side up, then upside down.

... until they were both so small that he could see neither one. Or anything for that matter.

... and the world got smaller ...

And as he fell, he watched
in amazement as the
school got smaller . . .

But when the doors closed behind him, he had no choice but to fall.

When it finally stopped, his bottom was sore from the rough ride, and when it came time to get off, he didn't know what to do. There was no place to step!

... on an upside-down school bus that hit every bump and every hole in the road along the way.

His father was too busy for anything but a pat on the
head and getting him off to school . . .

Only this time, it was on the wrong side of the plate!

... into the kitchen, where she served him his breakfast as usual.

So with a bit of a struggle, he left his room and followed her . . .

When he answered,
his mother yelled

"Breakfast!"

as she disappeared
down the stairs,
unaware that anything
was wrong.

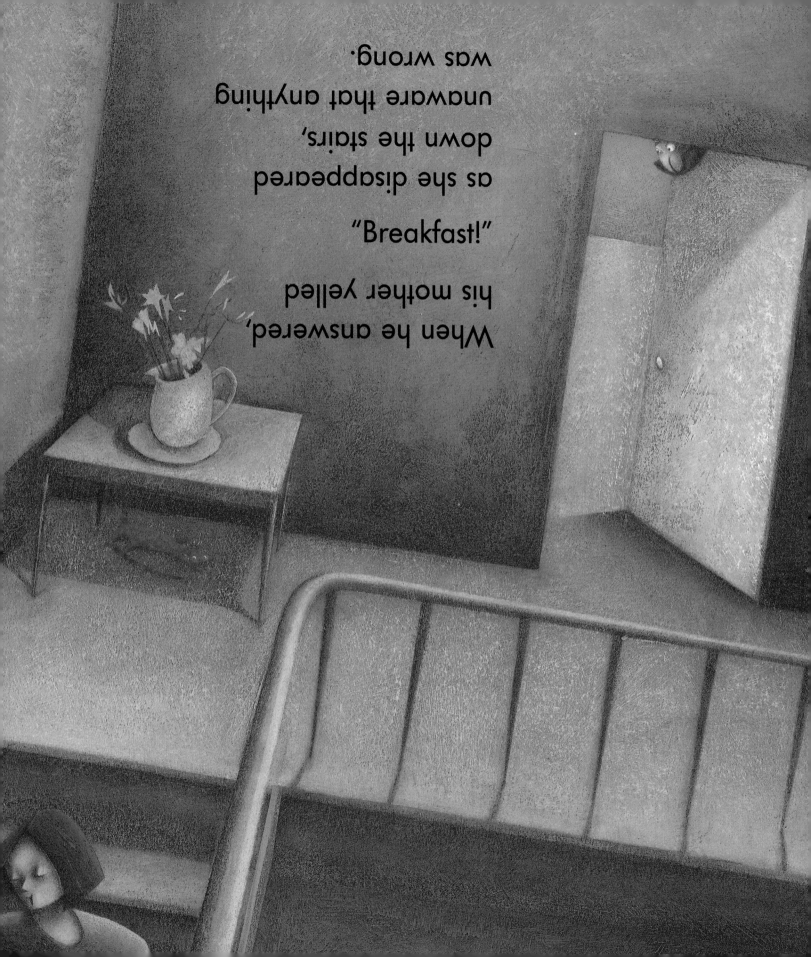

Suddenly, there was a knock at the door.

He could tell it was going to be one of those days.

was upside down!

The whole world

Moff rushed to the window and looked out.

If there is a left side,
then there is a right side,
and if there is a right side,
then there must be a wrong side, right?

the wrong side of the bed!

... he had gotten up on

And at that moment,
it became clear to
him what had actually
happened . . .

So over the edge he rolled and dropped and dropped and dropped until he came to a sudden stop.

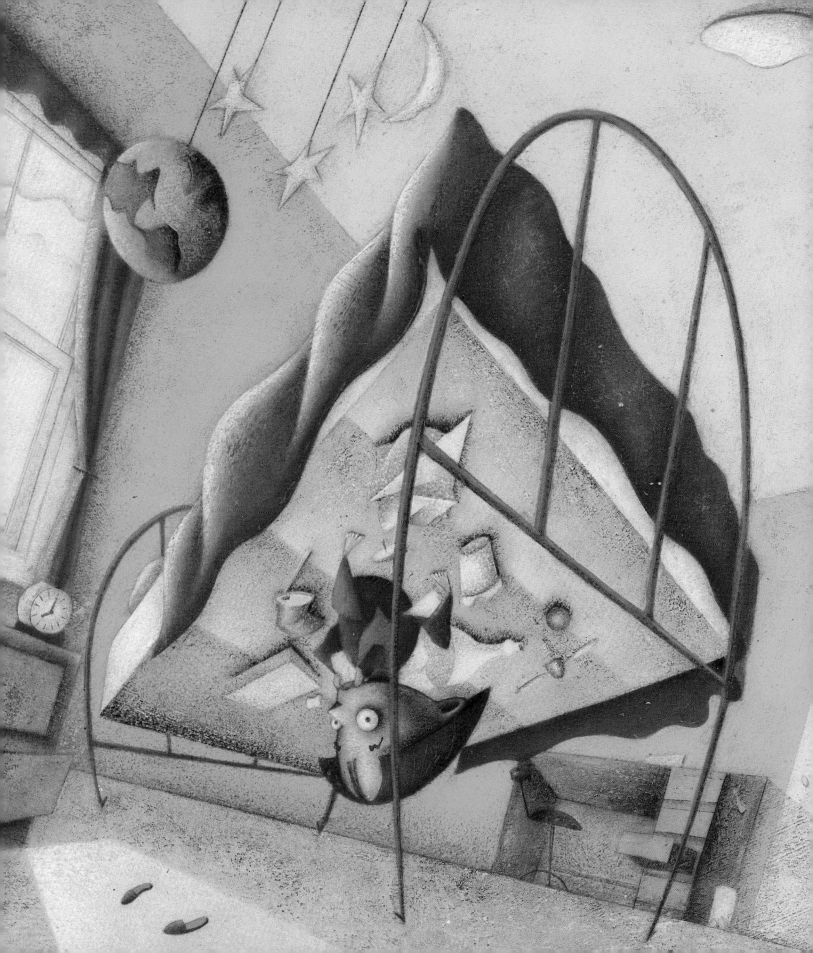

One morning little Mott Turner awoke confused and irritable and surrounded by everything under his bed. Nothing in his room looked familiar. It was time to get up!

# THE WRONG SIDE OF THE BED

BY WALLACE E. KELLER

CHILDREN'S UNIVERSE

Courtney,